HI, THERE – I'm Patty Mills.

I play basketball in the NBA, and I've represented Australia at the Olympics three times. That's these days. Growing up, I was a sports-loving kid just like you. And that's why I'm excited about my new series of kids' books, Game Day!

Patty, the main character, loves playing every sport he can – especially basketball. He learns many important skills and values through sports, dancing, and of course, at school. He also has a whole lot of fun with his friends, but when it comes to game day, he always makes sure he's ready to perform.

I think you're going to love taking this journey with Patty. Have fun reading the series, don't miss the glossary in the back of every book, and I hope to see you on the basketball court one day!

THE GAME DAY! SERIES

BOOK 1 *Patty Hits the Court*

BOOK 2 *Patty and the Shadows*

BOOK 3 *Patty Takes Charge*

First American Edition 2020
Kane Miller, A Division of EDC Publishing

Text copyright © Patty Mills and Jared Thomas 2017
Illustrations copyright © Nahum Ziersch 2017
First published in Australia in 2017 by Allen & Unwin.
Cover design by Ruth Grüner and Nahum Ziersch.
Text design and typesetting by Ruth Grüner.
Cover illustration by Nahum Ziersch.

For information contact:
Kane Miller, A Division of EDC Publishing
PO Box 470663
Tulsa, OK 74147-0663
www.kanemiller.com
www.edcpub.com
www.usbornebooksandmore.com

Library of Congress Control Number: 2019940424

Printed and bound in the United States of America

2 3 4 5 6 7 8 9 10

ISBN: 978-1-68464-022-5

BOOK 1

PATTY MILLS

WITH **JARED THOMAS**

ILLUSTRATIONS BY **NAHUM ZIERSCH**

Kane Miller
A DIVISION OF EDC PUBLISHING

CHAPTER 1

IT WAS THE THIRD-TO-LAST game of the footy season, and my time was running out.

"It's almost three-quarter time, let's really go for it," I told Boris, who was playing ruck. "Just tap it down to me."

My school footy team, St. Mary's, was playing against St. Joseph's, and I really wanted to beat my record.

I could get four goals in one game, I *knew* it – but I needed two more.

I could see it in my head: I'd step around a player, take a bounce, and then kick to tall, lean Manu at full-forward or Josie at center half-forward. If someone was about to tackle me, I'd dish it off to Tiago. His mop of shaggy black hair was easy to spot, and he was always in the right place at the right time.

Boris flashed me a cheeky smile as I caught my breath, waiting for the bounce. He launched his huge body into the air and tapped the ball straight into my hands. I burst around two of the St. Joseph's players, then handballed to Josie. Josie spun around to pass into full-forward, but when I yelled that I was in the clear, she looped the footy over to me with a gentle drop punt. I marked it.

I walked back to take my kick. I was about forty meters out from goal. I took a deep breath, dropped the ball onto my foot and booted through it as hard as I could.

It flew long and high, and split the center of the goals. I jumped up, punching the air. Boris ran over and lifted me off my feet. My other teammates slapped me on the back. Josie high-fived me. "You're going to smash your record, Patty," she said.

"Three down, one to go," I said.

AT THREE-QUARTER TIME I bit into a slice of orange as I sat listening to Coach Clarke give the team instructions. Coach Clarke was the coach of the basketball team, but that day he was filling in for Coach Riley. "Patty, I'm going to put you in the back pocket this quarter," he said.

I took the slice of orange from my mouth and looked up at him. "But I'm not tired. I could run all day!"

"I bet you could, Patty," Coach Clarke said, "but I'm going to give Tyson a go in the center this quarter."

I couldn't believe it. Tyson always beat me at athletics, but when it came to football, he couldn't touch me. When I'm on the ground I'm in my element – moving like the wind, my hands like magnets for the ball.

Tyson's not even a forward – he's a backline player. I knew Coach Clarke was only letting Tyson play in the center because he was the star player on the basketball team.

"Coach Clarke, I'm one goal away from beating my record," I pleaded.

"We're leading by five goals, Patty. Let's share it around a bit, hey, mate?"

Tyson grinned at me and said, "Don't worry, Patty. I'll boot a goal just for you."

I didn't want Tyson to kick a goal for me. And I didn't want to share my goals around. Scoring goals is what I love doing – it's what I'm really good at.

I sulked back onto the oval, knowing my chance to break my record was blown. I stood in the back pocket for what seemed like hours, watching Boris tap the ball down to Tyson. Like me, Tyson passed the ball to Manu, Tiago or Josie. Our team was so strong against St. Joseph's that it was like watching kick-to-kick. When Tyson kicked a goal I knew I should have been happy for him, but there was steam coming out of my ears.

It didn't help when Tiago threw his arm around me after the siren sounded and said, "Great game, Patty. Next time we play you should stay on the ball for the whole game."

Josie understood I was disappointed. She walked over and patted my shoulder just as Tyson jogged past.

"Pity you were stuck in the back pocket for the last quarter," he called.

"Well, at least you got to touch the ball for once."

Coach Clarke was congratulating my team-mates as they walked off the oval. "Nice work today, Patty," he said. Tiago was holding a bin full of footballs on top of his head, carrying them to the change rooms. I took the ball from beneath my arm and threw it. Somehow the ball landed in the bin, startling Tiago.

Coach Clarke took the ball out of the bin, told Tiago to stay standing where he was, threw it to me and said, "Do that again."

"Do what?" I asked him.

"Throw the ball into the bin."

I looked at Coach Clarke as if he was crazy, and threw the ball.

A smile spread across his face when the ball landed in the bin for the second time.

"Nice shooting," Tiago said with a laugh.

"Patty, have you ever thought about playing basketball?" Coach Clarke asked.

I shrugged my shoulders.

"I'd like you to try out," he said.

"Would I get to play on the ball for the whole game?" I asked him.

Coach Clarke laughed. "Everyone plays on the ball in basketball."

I thought about it as I walked into the change rooms. The basketball team was really strong: Boris, Manu and Tiago were all tall and skillful, and Tyson was a freak. They were expected to win their third grand final in a row.

2

I WAS ON THE OVAL with Boris, Manu, Tiago and Josie, sitting on my footy. I'd just finished eating my lunch, and Josie was looking at my snacks as if to tell me to eat the fruit I hadn't touched. I took the banana from my lunch box and began to peel it. Manu asked, "Can I have the rest of your snacks?" as he stuffed my pear into his mouth and took a handful of apricots.

As I bit into the banana and watched Manu pigging out, I saw Tyson walk toward the gym bouncing his basketball.

"Can you believe Tyson kicked a goal the other day?" I asked.

Boris, always reeling off statistics, said, "This year you've kicked a goal in every quarter where we're leading or only one goal down. That means it was almost certain that you would've kicked another goal, if you'd stayed on the ball."

I think Boris was trying to make me feel better about what had happened, but it wasn't working.

"I just want to play a team sport with you guys where I can always be a part of the action, and maybe one where we have a hope of playing in the finals."

"And how about a sport that gives us all the best chance of competing at the Olympics," Boris said.

"Yeah, but we'd be competing *against* each other!" I said. Boris, Manu and Tiago

12

had all moved to Australia because of
their parents' work, and we knew that
one day they'd return to their home countries.
None of us were sure how long we'd be living in
Canberra. Kids from all over the world came to
my school when their parents moved to Canberra
for work.

My dad's family is from the Torres Strait
Islands, and my mum's family is from the desert
country in South Australia. Boris is from Paris,
France. Manu is from Argentina. Sometimes when
he's frustrated he rants in Spanish. Tiago is from
Brazil; he speaks Portuguese, but always cracks
up when Manu curses in Spanish even though,
like me, I don't think he understands what Manu
is saying.

We all nodded at Boris's suggestion, and Josie said, "That'd be fun though. We definitely need to play a sport that gets us to the Olympics."

"Well, it's not running," Tiago said, "because you're too slow, Boris."

"And I don't want it to be swimming. Canberra is too cold and it's hard enough getting out of bed in the morning as it is. Swimmers start training at first light," Manu complained.

"You've got a swimmer's haircut," I said, running my hand across Manu's dark crew-cut hair.

"The thing that Boris and Tiago and I are best at is basketball," Manu declared.

"But I'm too short for basketball," I said.

"There are some really good Torres Strait

Islander basketballers," Josie said. I smiled because the basketball players Josie was talking about were my uncles, Sam and Danny. I'd seen photos and footage of them playing.

Boris looked at me and said, "You should come and try out, Patty. It's only fair – you're always getting us to try new things."

"Coach Clarke asked me to," I told them. "But your team is so strong, I'll just look silly."

"Two of our teammates are going on holidays in a few weeks – we need new players. You should come and have a try too, Josie," Tiago said.

"But what if we can't even bounce the ball?" I asked.

"You can bounce a football, right?" Boris asked.

"Yeah, of course I can."

"Well, a football is oval and a basketball is round, so the probability of you being able to bounce a basketball is very high," Boris told me.

I looked at Josie, who was packing her lunch box away. "Do you want to have a go?"

Josie lifted a shoulder and grinned. "I think we should. I'd love to play a team sport where we all get more of a go."

"Great!" said Manu. "We'll help train you up. We're counting on you being good, Patty and Josie, or else we've got no chance of winning our third grand final in a row."

"No pressure though?" Josie laughed.

I picked myself up off the oval and started following my friends across to the gym.

CHAPTER

3

TYSON SPUN AROUND to look at us as we walked into the gym. He stood in place, bouncing his basketball from hand to hand, and said, "Don't tell me you're going to play basketball, Patty! You're too short."

I shrugged. Coach Clarke walked over. "Tyson, keep practicing your layups," he boomed. Then he looked at me with a smile. "Glad you've taken up my offer, Patty. Good to see you too, Josie."

Coach Clarke looked like a giant standing on the court in his tracksuit.

"I thought it would be good to have a try," I said.

"Go and grab yourself a basketball each and run a few laps dribbling around the court."

"Dribbling?" Josie asked.

"Bouncing the ball," Coach Clarke explained.

I thought it sounded easy enough.

While Josie pulled her long curly hair into a ponytail, I took off. I found dribbling a whole lot easier than bouncing a football, but when I looked back to see how Josie was doing, I saw the ball hit the toe of her shoe and roll across the court.

She chased it and Tyson stamped his foot down on the ball. Josie reached and pried the ball from beneath his weight. "Come on, Josie, have another go," I told her.

Boris gave her an encouraging thumbs-up.

"Whoa, don't slip up now, Josie," Tyson laughed, but by the time she had run a lap around the court, she had gotten the hang of it, just as I knew she would.

When we finished running our laps Coach Clarke said, "Good work, guys," and waved us up to the free end of the court.

"Basketball is all about scoring points and stopping the other team from scoring," Coach Clarke explained. Josie launched the ball at the basket. It hit the hoop and bounced back, almost taking Coach Clarke's head off. "Easy, tiger," he said with a chuckle as he caught the ball in his huge hand. "No shooting yet, I just need you to listen. What I'd like you to work at is what's called a layup." Coach Clarke bounced the ball toward the basket and then threw it. It hit the board and dropped through the hoop.

"Can you see what I did there?" he asked.

"You scored a basket. Woo!" Josie answered, throwing her arms in the air.

"Thanks, Josie," he said with a smile, but then he turned serious. "But *how* did I score it?"

"By bouncing it off the board thing," I said.

"That's right. It's called the backboard. When you're doing a layup, if you run in on an angle

and get the ball to hit the top corner of the square on the backboard, the ball has the best chance of going in."

"It's at least twenty percent more likely to go in," Boris said.

Josie and I looked at each other and she rolled her eyes. Boris pulled these stats from nowhere sometimes. But still, it sounded easy enough.

"I want you to stand right here," Coach Clarke said, "and have a go at making the ball hit the corner of the square. The trick is making your upper arm parallel to the ground, and your forearm vertical, sitting the ball comfortably on your hand and balancing it with the other, then pushing the ball up."

Again Coach Clarke launched the ball toward the top of the square, hit the target and scored.

"Your turn now," he said.

Josie lined up first. She had a shot and it went

through the hoop. "Good, Josie," Coach Clarke said, "but that was more like a netball goal. I want you to try and get the ball in off the backboard."

She tried again, and did a little dance when the ball rebounded off the board and dropped through.

Then it was my turn. I looked up at the basket, and it seemed so far away. I was worried that I wouldn't be able to make the distance. I took a shot and it bounced off the hoop.

Coach Clarke passed the ball back to me. I tried again and it sailed high, hitting the top of the board and falling away. I felt blood rushing to my face. The rest of the team was watching me, and I noticed a smirk forming at the side of Tyson's mouth. I started to think that throwing

the football into the ball bin after the game had been a fluke.

On my next turn I really tried to make my shooting arm like Coach Clarke had shown us, steadying the ball with my free hand. This time I was closer, but it still didn't go in. I heard Tyson snicker and mutter something about my "goal-scoring record." I tried one more time, putting all of my feelings of embarrassment into my shot, and the ball hit the center of the square then rebounded straight back at me, hitting me in the chest. This time Tyson laughed loudly.

I slammed the ball onto the court and walked

away. Josie caught it as it bounced.

"Come on, Patty," Coach Clarke said, "it's just a matter of practice. You stay here and practice with Josie – you'll get there." And he took the rest of the team to the other end of the court to practice their defensive moves.

I was humiliated – I was never the one who struggled, playing any sport. But Josie didn't give me time to feel down. We took it in turns, and  by the end of ten minutes Josie had scored about twenty baskets. Although I had only scored two, she told me I was doing well.

Having Josie at the first tryout with me made me feel more confident. Josie is one of the best sportspeople I know. She's a whiz at netball and a really good footballer. She's tall, fast, strong and bumps and tackles just as hard as the boys. I'm also lucky that Josie is my best friend. Her parents moved to Canberra from the Torres Strait Islands at the same time as my family. She has always called me *"bala"* – brother – and cheers me up whenever I'm down. She never gives up and never lets me give up either.

Coach Clarke blew his whistle. "Okay, how about a scratch match."

"All right!" Tyson said, and the other players moved into the middle of the court.

We were split into teams of five players. Josie and I were teamed up with Adam, Nathan and Ben. We gathered in the center for the jump ball.

I felt silly. I didn't know where to stand, didn't

know the positions like I did in AFL and NRL, and Tyson told me, "When you get the ball, just run to the end of the court and make a try like you do in rugby league. But you better run as fast as you can because I'm going to catch you."

Nathan went in for the jump ball. He sometimes played ruck with Boris at footy, so I was prepared for him to tap it down to me.

When he did, I started running with the ball as fast as I could toward the basket. Coach Clarke blew his whistle and called out, "Travel," and made a signal with his hands, rolling one over the other.

Everyone was laughing at me, even Coach Clarke. I had no idea what was wrong until Coach explained, "You have to bounce the ball, Patty.

You can't run with it unless you're bouncing it."

Tyson ripped the ball out of my hands. "Let me take care of that for you," he said false sweetly. He passed it to Tiago and they were off.

When Coach Clarke blew the whistle at the end of the session, Tyson threw his arm around my shoulder and said, "Looks like I don't have to worry about you being better than me at basketball!"

I scowled at him, but couldn't think of a comeback. The truth was, he was right. Tyson was a star at basketball, and I was hopeless.

"You did well, Patty," Coach Clarke said. "So did Josie."

"You've got to be joking. I was awful."

"I'm not and you weren't awful. There's training again on Wednesday, I hope to see you back."

"Thanks but no thanks," I told him, keen to get to dance practice in the evening and start feeling good about myself again.

CHAPTER

4

I SLUMPED ONTO THE COUCH to watch television as Mum and Dad prepared dinner. Mum must have known something was wrong because she asked if I wanted a banana milkshake.

I'd been crazy about banana milkshakes since I had my first at Uncle Frankie's Café on Thursday Island in the Torres Strait. There's a sign at Uncle Frankie's that says, "The Best Shakes in the Straits," but Mum's shakes come close.

"Patty, did you hear me? Would you like a milkshake?" she asked again.

"No thanks, Mum." I'd just come from Torres Strait Islander dance practice, which usually

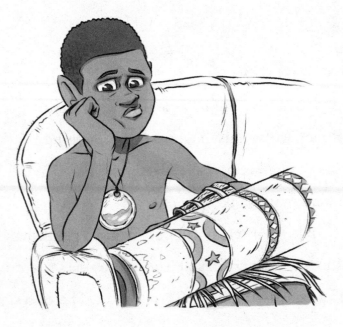

made me feel energized and positive, but I was still thinking about my basketball tryout.

Mum sat down next to me. "Okay, tell me what's wrong."

I shook my head and kept staring at the television.

"Why have you been moping around all afternoon?" Mum said, placing her hand on my shoulder.

"It's nothing, really."

"I know when something's wrong, Patty."

I sighed. "I tried out for basketball today, but I could hardly do anything."

Mum laughed, but it wasn't funny to me. "So, you want to be a basketballer like your Uncle Danny?"

33

"I thought I might be good at it. I wanted to get on the team and help my friends win their third grand final in a row."

"Hmm," she said, and shot me the serious look she gives me when she wants me to think long and hard about something.

"I was hopeless."

"You couldn't bounce the ball? You couldn't pass it? You kept tripping over your feet?" Mum asked.

"Pretty much."

"You couldn't catch the ball like you do in football and cricket and rugby league?" Mum asked.

I started to think Mum was making fun of me. "Of course I could. But I couldn't shoot the ball, and when we played a scratch match I didn't even know where to stand on the court."

Mum walked over to the bookshelf and took down the photo of Uncle Danny in his Australian basketball team uniform. She placed it in front of me on the coffee table. "Do you think Uncle Danny was good at basketball when he first started playing?" she asked.

"I don't know, but at least he would've been tall."

"All giants were growing boys like you at one time, Patty," Mum said. "And I'll let you in on a secret." She leaned in close to me. "Uncle Danny was dropped from his primary school basketball team."

"You're joking!" I said.

"Ask him yourself," Mum said, chuckling.

"Really?"

"It's true, Patty," Mum said. "He wasn't very good at basketball when he first played – he was better at athletics. You're already great at all of the other sports you play, imagine how good you might be at basketball if you practice."

I wasn't convinced. Perhaps basketball was going to be the one sport I wasn't good at.

But Mum wasn't finished. "You have to have the confidence to push through the early stages, while you're learning. Don't expect to set the court on fire straightaway! But if you keep trying, you'll get there. Just like you have with your other  sports. Just like with your Torres Strait dancing."

As I tried to sleep that night I thought about what it felt like when I introduced our Torres Strait Islander dance group, Gerib Sik, to an audience. I stood straight and tall, and my voice boomed out. Then, when we danced, I moved smoothly across the floor like a shark gliding through the ocean. It hadn't always been that way; it had taken a while to learn the steps. But I had gotten there. And now it was the best feeling in the world.

CHAPTER 5

"YOU WANT TO HAVE another go at basketball training today?" I asked Josie when the bell went for lunch.

"I was going to have a go whether you wanted to or not," Josie said. "I've been using my netball as a basketball and practicing at home."

We scoffed our sandwiches and shot straight over to the gym.

I watched Tyson dribbling the ball around the court. He looked really relaxed. I remembered what Mum said: I wasn't good at basketball yet, but I *could* be, if I tried. I just had to have the confidence to ignore Tyson.

He wasn't going to make it easy, though. He shot over a comment as he jogged past. "Patty, you're still as short as last time you came to practice."

"*Eres un estúpido*, Tyson," Manu said.

Tiago started giggling and Tyson asked, "What?"

Manu replied, "I said Patty is tall enough." But I knew what he'd really said. I squashed down a smile.

We all ran a few laps dribbling before Coach

Clarke called us to the end of the court. "Okay, let's see your layups now."

When it came to my turn, I dribbled the ball, then pushed it up toward the corner of the backboard square, making sure to balance it with my free hand.

The ball dropped through the hoop, and I punched the air, so glad that I'd got it. When I walked back up the line Josie gave me a high five.

I was pumped when it came to playing a scratch match. "Can you tell us some of the rules again before we start?" I asked Coach Clarke.

Tyson rolled his eyes, but I let Mum's words calm the anger that rose up in me. *If you keep*

trying, you'll get there. Someday soon I'd be blocking Tyson when he tried to take a shot.

"Okay, how about we all take a few minutes to teach our new teammates the rules?" Coach Clarke said. Josie smiled at me when he said "new teammates."

Nathan explained some of the rules to us, including that a free throw was worth one point, and that you could score three points by getting a basket from outside the three-point line.

I looked at how far the basket was from the line and imagined one day being able to shoot a three-pointer.

Manu and Nathan stood toe-to-toe for the jump ball. Nathan won it and tapped the ball

down to me. I started dribbling toward our team's
end, and Tyson ran in and defended. Certain that
he was going to slap the ball out of my hands,

I stepped backward. Josie and Nathan were
calling out to me and waving their arms
around, but I decided to take Tyson on. I ran
around him as fast as I could, and the ball
was bouncing up around my head. I didn't
care. I just wanted to get to the basket.

Charlie tried to stop me but I dodged
him, and when I felt the ball was going to

slip out of my hand I took a
shot.

The ball dropped through
the hoop. "Yes!" I yelled, and
punched the air. But when

I looked around at my teammates, Nathan was shaking his head.

"What?"

"You've got to pass it," he said.

"Why? I scored," I told him.

Tyson scowled at me as he ran past, but that didn't make me any less happy about scoring my first basket in a game, even if it was just a scratch match.

Tyson turned and said, "It was just a fluke, Patty." So the next time I got the ball I did the same thing. I sped toward the basket, dodging Tyson and Ben, but when I shot the ball, it missed altogether.

"Argh!" I said to myself in frustration. I had to prove my shot wasn't a fluke.

Next time I charged to the hoop and tried throwing the ball up when I was as close as I could get to the basket.

The ball bounced off the hoop, and I slapped my leg, totally annoyed with myself. Tyson caught the rebound, dribbled it back to his end of the court and scored.

I told myself that when I next got hold of the ball I needed to concentrate harder. But I missed on my next attempt too, and I heard Josie and Nathan groan.

Coach Clarke blew the whistle. When everyone was at the drinking fountain he came to me and said, "Patty, you have to work with your teammates. Basketball is a team game."

My face went hot. I didn't know what Coach

Clarke was talking about. I knew basketball was a team game, but like most sports, I thought you won the game by scoring points, not by passing the ball around.

I thought that Coach Clarke was just being tough on the new kid, but then my friends started giving me a hard time too.

"Didn't you see me calling out to you, Patty?" Josie asked. She hardly ever got annoyed with anyone, especially me, but there was a deep frown on her face.

"You could have dressed like a bullfighter waving a red flag and Patty wouldn't have seen you," Tiago said.

CHAPTER 6

THERE ARE A LOT OF THINGS I like about school – seeing my friends, doing PE, learning about geography. I'm good at remembering facts. Sometimes I'm okay at math and English, and other times they're really difficult. I have to concentrate so hard to get it right.

If it's a rainy day at school we have to play board games in the library at lunchtime. On days like that, when I don't get to run around, it's even harder for me to concentrate.

Sometimes, when it's freezing cold in Canberra, I sit in class dreaming about being on Thursday Island, where my grandparents and lots of my family live. We go there for holidays. It's always sunny on Thursday Island, and I spend the days hanging out with my cousins.

We can walk or ride bikes wherever we want on the island and we walk around barefoot in shorts and tank tops. It's so much better than being in a classroom wearing school shoes and having the collar of my shirt rubbing against my neck.

We swim and play on the beach, and a lot of the time we dive. There's reef everywhere in the

Torres Strait, and I always dream about diving.

The water is crystal clear and the sun shines through it, lighting up the reef. Everything is silent under the water as I glide along, sometimes following a school of mullet, a stingray, or if I'm really lucky, a turtle or a small reef shark or two.

Sitting in my English class that afternoon, my mind drifted away from what the teacher was saying. I started thinking about what Coach Clarke had said about basketball being a team game. Sure, I had scored a basket, but Tyson was right – it had been a fluke. When I was playing football and rugby and knew I couldn't score, I'd pass the ball to someone in a better position, knowing that there were times that I couldn't possibly break through the defense by myself. I guessed that was what Coach Clarke wanted me to do.

I didn't know how I was going to pass the ball to Tyson though, once we were playing a real game. Even if our team was losing, it would be hard.

And then my teacher, Ms. Kelly, placed her hand on my desk. "Patty, I haven't seen you do any work for the last five minutes," she said, "and the results of this test prove that you need to work much harder. I'm going to have to speak with your parents."

"Sorry, Miss," I said, looking at the result of my spelling test. My score was seven out of twenty. Mum and Dad were going to freak.

I looked back down at the page with the comprehension exercises and spelling words that I was supposed to be practicing and started to stress out.

Josie caught my attention and mouthed the words, "What's wrong?"

I held up the paper just long enough for her to

see the mark, and she held her head in her hands. We all dreaded not getting at least fourteen out of twenty on a test. It meant that I'd be kept in to study in the classroom instead of playing Friday afternoon sports.

I **WALKED HOME** from school every day. I was supposed to do chores like emptying the dishwasher and tidying my bedroom, though I didn't always remember. That night I definitely remembered. I even threw some clothes in the washing machine and fed our cat, Cupid, before Mum and Dad got home and took me out for our regular pizza night.

I sat at the restaurant with my mouth watering, cutting a slice of Hawaiian pizza with the stretchiest cheese and juiciest pineapple, when Dad asked, "Did you have another try at basketball, Patty?"

"I went to training at lunchtime today," I said.

"And how was it?"

"I dribbled past everyone and made a layup."

"That's great," Mum said. But even though Mum and Dad were pleased and I had bitten into the best pizza in the world, I still felt sick thinking about my spelling test result. I knew I had to come out with it.

"Mum and Dad, I didn't pass the spelling test this week."

"What's going on, Patty?" Dad asked. "Are there certain words you're finding difficult?"

"Not all of them, just some," I said.

"Maybe you need to pull back on some of the extra things you're doing outside of school," Mum said.

"There's no way I'm missing dance rehearsals," I told them, shaking my head.

"Well, you'll have to miss out on football this week, Patty," Mum said.

I looked to Dad and said, "That's not fair."

"You know the rule, Patty. If you're behind on schoolwork you can't play sports on Friday afternoon."

"But I don't want to miss out on playing football! Can't you just speak to Ms. Kelly? I promise

I'll work harder at my spelling," I begged. I knew that Coach Clarke would put Tyson straight onto the ball if I wasn't playing, and I'd end up in the back pocket for our last game.

"Patty, improving your spelling is more important than football at the moment," Dad said.

I bit into my pizza, which didn't taste as good as it had a few minutes ago. Dad went on to ask, "What can we do about it?"

"How about you speak to Ms. Kelly, tell her I can play football, and I'll practice spelling with you all weekend."

Dad chuckled and said, "Patty, you're not playing football on Friday. You'll have to do revision with Ms. Kelly instead."

"But, Dad!" I couldn't believe they were being so hard on me.

And Mum said, "Patty, I don't want you to spend all of your weekend practicing your spelling. It's about doing a little bit of practice each day and concentrating more in class."

"Yeah, but I won't be able to play football, will I? And I bet I won't be able to play basketball, even if Coach Clarke selects me for the team." I felt like my world was falling apart.

"Patty, you could be on top of your school-work in no time. How about you try thinking about what your education means to your future rather than trying to get a good enough result to play sports? An education will provide you with the greatest range of options to do whatever you want with your life. I know there are other things you dream of doing, Patty. Like managing a Torres Strait dance group one day."

I thought about what Dad was saying as I bit into my pizza.

"And if you get on top of your schoolwork, of course you'll be able to play basketball," Mum said.

"HAVE FUN, PATTY," Tyson said as he and my friends went to play sports. I was stuck sitting in the classroom. I just hoped that Tyson didn't kick a bag of goals.

After a while I looked down at my new word list and realized there were too many words on the page that I didn't know how to spell.

Although I really wanted to get on top of my schoolwork to play football and basketball, I thought about what Dad had said about my future.

When I grew up, I wanted to manage a Torres Strait Islander dance group. You need to know a lot of things when you manage a dance group. I remember the last time Dad and my Uncle Noel took our group on a tour. First they needed to book the performances in different towns and cities. They needed to know how much we were being paid for each performance, hire a bus for our travel, book our accommodation and make sure that we were all fed. To be a manager, you need to know how to plan and be organized, negotiate and communicate, and those are all skills that education helps to build.

I realized I needed to switch on in class to give myself a chance at being the best I could be.

Ms. Kelly came and sat next to me. "Patty, read the word first and then spell it out."

She told me to cover the word with a ruler and write it down in my book, then uncover it to see if I'd spelled it correctly.

The first word I tried was "privilege." It had me stumped. I spelled it out as P-R-I-V-I-L-E-G-E, but for some reason when I wrote it down, I kept putting a *D* before the *G*.

I lay down my pen and took a breath. Ms. Kelly asked, "Is there anything that can help you remember how to spell the word?"

It wasn't as easy as just telling myself not to add a *D*. I knew how to spell "edge" and kept getting it confused with "privilege."

I looked at the *D* and the *G* in the word and said to Ms. Kelly, "*G* is for goal and *D* is for defense. Without defense it's easier to score a goal, and scoring a goal is a privilege."

She grinned. "That's good, Patty. Keep practicing and I'll come back in a minute."

I ran through the little riddle I'd made up a few times, looked at the word, covered it and then tried writing it down.

When I uncovered the word and saw that I'd spelled it correctly, I punched the air. "Yes!" I said, and Ms. Kelly looked across to me and asked, "Got it, Patty?"

I nodded. "Keep it going!" she said.

I made a game of it. Each word I learned to spell was a basketball goal. I was excited to tell Dad and Mum my score.

CHAPTER 7

"HEY, PATTY," Josie and Tiago said when I leaned my bike up against a tree at the park. I was super keen to start practicing. "Where are Manu and Boris?" I asked.

"Maybe they slept in," Tiago said.

"Don't you mean Boris is stuck waiting for Manu to finish eating a gigantic breakfast?" Josie replied.

"Probably," I said. Manu loved to eat. But then I saw them in the distance, riding along the path.

They parked their bikes and Manu said, "Let's practice some layups."

"See how many we can get in a row," Boris called out.

I felt self-conscious, remembering my disastrous run of layups at the first training session. But again I remembered what Mum had told me – if I kept trying, I would get there in the end.

My first shot went in and I realized I'd been holding my breath. When I scored my second I started to enjoy myself.

Trying to make a lot of baskets made us slow

down and concentrate on what we were doing. We shot fifteen baskets in a row: three each.

"Great shooting," Boris said. I tried to keep the smile off my face, but I was so pleased with myself.

Boris, Manu and Tiago started competing for the rebounds so I tried to get into position too, but they kept blocking me out. It seemed like none of them were going to share the ball with me.

Tyson rode over to the court on his BMX.

He sat slumped over his handlebars for a couple of minutes before he called out, "Can you get the ball to reach the hoop yet, Patty?"

"I've scored more than you did yesterday, Tyson," I answered, knowing he'd only kicked a point in the footy match and was moved from rover to the back pocket at halftime.

"Well, at least I got a better spelling test result than you," Tyson teased.

Boris jumped in. "We just made fifteen layups in a row."

"Who did, *Patty*?" Tyson asked. I smirked at Tyson thinking I could have improved so quickly.

"No, we shot three each," Boris said.

"Right," Tyson said, scratching his head. "Okay, who's ready for half-court three on three?" He dropped his bike. "You're on my team, Tiago, and you too, Boris," he announced.

Tyson threw the ball to me. "First team to twenty points wins."

I moved to the center of the court. Tyson got into position to pressure me as I attempted to get the ball to Josie and Manu.

I wanted Josie to go to the far right side of the court, but I couldn't just call out and tell her where to go – it would give my plan away.

My mind went to my dance group, which Josie was a member of too. Sometimes when we were learning a new dance, Uncle Noel would tap his hip to tell us which direction to move. I looked at Josie and when I knew she was watching me, I tapped my hip like Uncle Noel. Tyson wouldn't have had any idea what I was doing, but I was pleased when Josie moved to the far right.

I started to dribble the ball, at first moving to the left side of the court. I knew that Tyson would try to press up on me at some stage, but I thought I'd dribble the ball as far as I could before he made his move. I was about to pass to Josie when I thought I saw a clear path to the basket. I went for it, only to be blocked easily by Tiago just as the ball left my hands. I looked sheepishly back at Josie, but she was looking at Manu; they were both frowning.

It seemed like only seconds later when Tiago scored, and a minute after that it was Tyson.

I dribbled the ball back to the center of the court then passed to Manu.

As soon as he had it, he gave it to Josie – then they just passed it back and forth between themselves. Even when I was standing in the clear, jumping up and down and calling to them, they wouldn't pass the ball to me. I started to wonder if they thought I was hopeless... and then I remembered how mad they had been with me when I wouldn't share the ball in our scratch match. And I'd just done the same thing again.

"Come on, guys," I said to them when Tyson took the ball back to the center of the court. "Why won't you pass it to me?"

"I didn't see you there," Manu said.

"I've learned my lesson. If I get the ball I'll pass it around. I promise."

"Are you sure?" Josie asked.

I nodded, and next time when Manu

approached the basket he bolted around
Tyson and passed the ball to me. I passed
it back to him before Tiago could block
him, and Manu made a layup.

"That's the way," Josie said, giving us
both high fives.

Tyson didn't look happy that I'd assisted
Manu. It made me happy though, and I knew
I could do it again.

So next time I had the ball, I didn't even
think about trying to score myself – I just tried to
pass to Manu and Josie, making the most of their
height and skill.

I bounce-passed the ball to Josie through
Tyson's legs, and she spun around and scored.
A few minutes later I did a no-look pass to Manu

that led to another basket and completely rattled Tiago, Boris and Tyson.

IN THE END we lost twenty points to twelve, but at least Josie and Manu scored three baskets each, and we got to see Tyson's moves.

I'd make sure to remember and practice them for the next time we played, and keep working on my shooting so that I could contribute to our score in the future.

Afterward, Josie and I sat on the lawn having a drink. Satisfied that he'd beaten us by so much, Tyson said, "You guys did all right. Keep practicing every day and you'll be ready for our first game."

"When's that?" Josie asked.

"Against St. Joseph's in two weeks."

"You think we'll make the team?" Josie asked excitedly.

Tyson shrugged and said, "That's up to Coach Clarke," before he rode off on his BMX.

CHAPTER

8

"I'VE GOT AN IDEA," I told Josie as we started riding home to my place for lunch. "Let's go to the library and get some books about basketball."

Josie agreed. "But you've got to let me help you with your spelling homework. There's no way I'm playing my first game of basketball without you."

We started looking in the sports section of

the library, and I found a book called *Basketball: Steps to Success*. As soon as I held up the cover to show Josie she said, "That's exactly what we need."

"Josie," I asked, feeling embarrassed, "can you show me some good books to read that might help me with my spelling?"

"For sure, *bala*!" she answered with a smile.

"HI, JOSIE, hi, Patty," Mum and Dad said when we walked into my lounge room.

"How was basketball practice?" Dad asked.

"Awesome," Josie said. "But we need to practice a lot more to get ready for our first game."

"Your first game?" Mum asked.

"The season starts in two weeks," Josie told her.

Mum looked at us and asked, "And you're on the team, Patty?"

"It's up to Coach Clarke, but we're practicing as much as we can to improve," Josie explained as we sat down at the kitchen table.

"But, Patty, remember, if you're not up on your schoolwork you won't be playing basketball."

"I haven't forgotten about that, Mum," I told her. How could I? "That's why Josie is here, to help me with my spelling homework."

Mum raised an eyebrow and said, "Ms. Kelly will be watching how you do very closely over the next couple of weeks."

"I'll make sure he gets on top of it," Josie said.

"What's this?" Dad asked, picking up the basketball book.

"We thought we'd get some tips," I told him.

"Good thinking," Dad said, and then he turned to Mum and said, "Maybe basketball is going to help Patty with his schoolwork. When was the last time he borrowed a book from the public library?"

Mum shrugged her shoulders and gave a little smile.

"And, Dad, after Josie has helped me with my homework, can we watch some footage of Uncle Danny playing?" I asked him.

"Sure," he said, "but eat some of my chicken soup first, you must be starving!"

AFTER LUNCH, Dad went outside and Josie and I went to the study. Josie opened the basketball book. "Read it aloud, Patty," she said. "If there are any words you don't know we'll look them up in the dictionary. It'll be good for your spelling."

Dad started up with his drill outside, and we closed the window so we could concentrate. We learned more about playing defense, and that dribbling strongly with both hands is important for changing direction on the court and evading the opposition. I also learned how to spell some new words, like "attempt," "pivot," "regulation," and by looking in the dictionary, the difference between "stationary" and "stationery."

After we ran through my spelling lists we sat on the couch, and Dad showed us footage of Uncle Danny playing for the Brisbane Bullets. It was the game that got them into the grand final against the Perth Wildcats. Dad explained that at

this point, Uncle Danny was coming to the end of his career, but he still shot fifteen points playing off the bench.

I felt a ball of energy burning inside me as I watched Uncle Danny score the final basket to beat the Wollongong Hawks. I knew that I wanted more than anything to be the greatest basketballer I could be.

And then Dad said, "Come and have a look outside."

We walked out to the driveway to discover that Dad had put up a basketball backboard.

"It's awesome! I'm going to practice fifty layups every morning before school," I told Dad and Josie, all fired up after watching Uncle Danny.

CHAPTER 9

I WAS MORE NERVOUS before my spelling test the next Wednesday morning than I'd ever been before a game of football. To relax, I thought about all the revision I'd done. Ms. Kelly called out the first word – "talent" – and I started to spell it out, remembering that it didn't have two *L*s.

I punched the air when Ms. Kelly

handed me back my result later that afternoon. I'd scored eighteen out of twenty.

Boris jumped out of his chair and slapped me on the back. "You've got your chance to kick four goals!" he said. But Ms. Kelly gave him a stern look and he sat back down.

I DIDN'T KICK FOUR GOALS in my last football match of the season, but I did keep my promise to Mum and Dad to focus on my schoolwork.

At the end of the last basketball training session before the start of the season, Coach Clarke pulled us all together and said, "I'm proud of how hard you've all worked in the lead-up to the season, and I'm particularly proud of Patty and Josie." Then he handed us each a team jersey. We were smiling from ear to ear as our teammates applauded.

It was so hard to concentrate in class on the morning leading up to my first basketball game. Dad and Mum were taking the afternoon off to watch, and I couldn't wait to wear the new light- and dark-blue jersey that looked like the ones professional teams wore.

When I felt my mind wandering during class, I took a moment to think about the things Dad had told me about the importance of education. Then I turned my attention back to Ms. Kelly. She was teaching us about the Australian political system in preparation for an excursion to Parliament House.

Our basketball game was after lunch so to conserve our energy during the break, Boris, Tiago, Josie and I sat on the edge of the oval and watched everyone play footy. But Manu, who never runs out of energy, decided to join the game. We kept ourselves entertained by cheering our friends on.

 "Holding the ball," Tiago yelled out whenever Manu got hold of it

even for a second, and we all cracked up.

When the lunch bell went, the team lined up for the school bus to St. Joseph's.

I'd played football on their oval but had never been in their school gym before. It was a lot like ours, but bigger, with a couple more courts. There was an electronic scoreboard placed high on the wall at one end.

When we had changed into our uniforms and stepped onto the court, Coach Clarke said, "It's time to warm up, team. Let's start with some layups, but take it easy."

It felt like I was floating as I dribbled toward the basket. The ball bounced off the backboard and dropped straight through the hoop.

When I turned to run back to the line I saw Dad and Mum. Dad gave me the thumbs-up and Mum waved at me. They walked over to Coach Clarke and introduced themselves, then took a seat in the stands.

Dad and Mum loved watching me play sports and I was feeling even more pumped about the game because they were there.

After I'd done another layup, Josie and I looked at the kids at the other end of the court. "They're tall, aren't they, Patty?" Josie said, and all I could do was nod in agreement. I'd get thrashed by them.

"You're tall," I reminded Josie. "And quick."

"And you're smart, fast and skillful," she said to me. I smiled. She couldn't pretend I was tall –

but I had to have confidence that my other skills would get me through.

Coach Clarke pulled us into a huddle a couple of minutes before the game started. "Thank you, Patty and Josie, for joining our team this season. I can see that you're going to be great basketball players. It's important in this game not to expect too much from yourselves. Just get used to playing, listen to the referee and me, and enjoy the game. I'm going to rotate players often, giving everyone plenty of court time. Okay, Boris, I want you to inbound the ball, and Tyson, you're point guard. Patty, Josie and Charlie, you're starting. Stand next to a player roughly your own height and good luck."

I walked into the center of the court.

My heart was pounding as I picked out a player to stand by. The shortest St. Joseph's player was still much taller than me.

My palms were sweating and I wiped them on my jersey. *What am I doing here? I'm not a basketball player,* I thought. The referee blew his whistle.

I tried to set up in a good position, but my opponent was all over me. Tyson broke away from his player and Charlie passed to him for an easy layup. Much as I hated to admit it, it was easy to see why Tyson was the star of the team.

Our supporters and my teammates on the bench thumped their feet on the floor in celebration. It was the first time I'd heard that sound and I loved it.

But a lot can happen in only a few seconds in basketball; we didn't set up our defense in time and the opposition scored.

I needed to do something before Coach Clarke benched me. I was standing just outside the key as Boris shot the ball. Everyone raced toward the basket, but the ball hit the hoop, bounced over their heads and right into my hands. Charlie screened his player so I could have a clear shot. I could hear everyone yelling, "Shoot it, Patty!"

Although I rushed a little, I felt confident, remembering to push the ball up properly like I'd practiced every morning before school. The ball hit the backboard and dropped in the hoop.

"Nice one," Boris said, tapping my hand as he ran past. I could feel the vibrations of the stomping feet through the court, and I knew this time it was for me. Getting my first basket felt even better than scoring in football.

Coach Clarke called time-out and everyone patted each other's backs in the huddle. Josie, Charlie and I were benched as Nathan, Manu and Tiago jogged onto the court, but all I could think about was getting my hands on the ball again and driving to the basket.

Dad and Mum caught my eye and gave me another thumbs-up when I was subbed back on.

"Boris, Boris," I called out as soon as he had the ball. He passed it to me and I dribbled toward the basket with ease.

One of the opposition players ran in front of me, so I shot the ball. It bounced off the hoop and Tyson grumbled, "Slow it down, Patty." But it was like I was possessed.

The next time the ball was in my hands my teammates were scattering around our key as the opposition applied heavy pressure. I was getting flustered, wanting to try and make a layup but knowing I should pass. I eventually passed to where I thought Manu was standing, but the ball was intercepted.

Manu was shaking his head and ranting in Spanish. "What?" I asked, and then a time-out was called and I was subbed off.

"Patty, watch what your teammates are doing," Coach Clarke instructed.

I sat on the bench feeling embarrassed by my mistake. I just wasn't cut out for basketball.

When there were only a few minutes left in the game, St. Joseph's were leading by a point. Coach Clarke told me to get ready. "Focus, Patty," he said, before I ran back on.

I raced around trying to get into a good position to receive the ball, but I never seemed to be in the right place at the right time.

I felt like walking off the court and giving up, but then the ball bounced off someone's shoe and rolled out to me.

I was just outside the key. I looked up to find someone to pass it to, but my teammates started yelling, "Shoot it, shoot it!"

I was confused. I turned my head to see what

Coach Clarke wanted me to do, and he was yelling "Shoot it, Patty!" too.

When I finally shot the ball, the siren

sounded. My shot didn't even reach the basket and the game was over. St. Joseph's beat us thirty to twenty-nine.

As I walked off the court, Tyson pointed to the scoreboard and said, "You have to watch the clock, Patty. Pass quickly to a shooter or have a shot yourself."

My teammates all walked off the court, looking at the ground. I didn't know if they were just angry because we lost our first game, or angry at me, but Tiago came across and said, "Your timing and focus were just a bit off, Patty. It's okay, you will get better."

Tyson was shaking his head, and even Josie wouldn't look me in the eye. I looked up into the crowd and saw my parents giving me encouraging smiles, but I knew I could have played much better.

Coach spoke to us. "It's clear that you all have different talents, and when you bring them together, you'll be a great team."

The others all walked off to their parents, but I stayed next to Coach Clarke. "I don't think I have any talents to bring to the team," I said.

"Patty, if you can play basketball half as well as you play other sports, you'll be great. Like I said before, you're just learning. We need you to make your best contribution for now, rather than trying to be the best player on the team."

I nodded, and started to walk over to Mum and Dad. Coach called after me, "Just stick at it, Patty."

CHAPTER 10

THE NEXT MONDAY was dance practice with my group, Gerib Sik. I was looking forward to taking my mind off basketball for a while.

When we danced we wore a grass skirt over our shorts called a *zazi*, and bands made of fiber around our legs, called *tetermus*. Even though it was only practice, it was still very serious.

Uncle Noel sat on the stage with his drum, which we call a *buru buru*. Dad and the uncles in charge of the chanting sat next to him.

Uncle Noel started beating the *buru buru* and we moved into our positions, our legs pumping up and down to the beat of the drum and the chanting. We held our left arms out straight and our right arms bent at the elbow and to the side, and started to move like sharks gliding through the reef.

When I'm dancing it feels like the rest of the world disappears. I feel peaceful and in control. But when I first started learning the different dances and their steps I felt hesitant and uncoordinated. I needed to practice a lot before I became good at them.

After the boys' first dance, Josie and the other Torres Strait girls walked on stage to move into position. Wanting to make sure the girls had their space to rehearse without interruption, I helped the younger boys settle down against the back wall of the rehearsal space, reminding them to be quiet and respectful. It was then that I realized I was a big part of the team with Gerib Sik. I knew that I could become a good member of my basketball team too, if I put my mind to it.

On the drive home Mum said, "You have great timing and control when you dance, Patty. You're aware of everyone around you, the beat of the music, and you move at exactly the right time."

From the expression on her face, I could tell she knew what I was thinking. "You're saying

I can use that skill playing basketball, aren't you?" I said.

She just smiled at me and winked.

CHAPTER

11

OUR SECOND GAME was being played at home. Stepping onto the court at my own school helped me feel a little less nervous. I looked up at the scoreboard and reminded myself to keep an eye on the time.

Coach Clarke called us into the huddle a couple of minutes before the game. "This week I want Tyson, Patty, Manu, Tiago and Josie to start. Manu, you take the jump ball and Josie, I want you to be under the basket at both ends of the court for rebounds. Patty, I want you to bring the ball down with Tyson and pass it to one of our forwards as soon as they're clear. Only shoot when you're in the key."

I didn't even think about shooting, but was happy to help Tyson bring the ball down, always looking up to see if my teammates were free.

The first move I made was when I noticed Josie standing clear near the three-point line and Tiago under the basket. I made it look like I was going to pass to Josie but lobbed a pass up for Tiago, and he scored easily.

Tiago patted me on the back when we ran back into defense.

My next play was driving toward the basket but, knowing Tyson was in the clear behind me, sneakily flicking the ball back to him to shoot.

"Yes!" I said when the ball dropped through.

"Thanks, Patty, I owe you one," Tyson said.

Coach Clarke's strategy worked well. We won forty points to twenty-five and Josie made six baskets, four of them from rebounds. Although I only scored two points from an easy layup, I was so happy that we'd won our first game and that I'd helped.

I was especially pleased that Manu stopped cursing me in Spanish.

OUR TEAM WAS constantly improving as we practiced during recess and lunchtimes, after school, on weekends and at training. It all paid off when we played, and we won six out of the next seven games.

Our basketball season was coming to an end, and we had made the semifinals against St. Michael's. The whole school was excited for us. Our class had even made a banner in the art room.

After dinner the night before the game, Dad said, "Why don't we watch a game of basketball before bedtime?"

"For sure," I answered.

Mum sat down with us, and Cupid jumped onto my lap and started purring. Dad put on Australia versus Russia at the Olympics. I had no idea who had won, but I badly wanted victory for Australia.

I could feel myself climbing up the back of the lounge chair in the last thirty seconds of the game. Australia was behind by only two points. I kept covering my eyes, worried that they were going to lose.

With only four seconds left, one of the Australian players passed the ball to the player waiting outside the three-point line. He jumped straight into the air as soon as he received the ball and shot. The ball swished through the basket, and the three of us jumped out of our chairs in celebration. Cupid cried out a ferocious meow before darting out of the room.

It was the best game I'd ever seen. If the Australian player hadn't passed to his teammate to shoot the three-pointer, Australia would have lost. It made me understand why teamwork was so important, especially in basketball.

When we settled down, Mum and Dad gave me a hug. "Sleep well, Patty," Mum said.

"You'll be great tomorrow," said Dad. "Get some rest."

BEFORE I TURNED OFF my bedside lamp I looked at my poster of Cathy Freeman. I thought about how nervous she must have been before she raced in the four hundred meters final at the 2000

Olympics in Sydney. Everyone in Australia was watching her, wanting her to win. My basketball game was nothing by comparison, but still, I would try to be like her – stay focused, and do my best. It was small-time games now, but you never knew where you might end up.

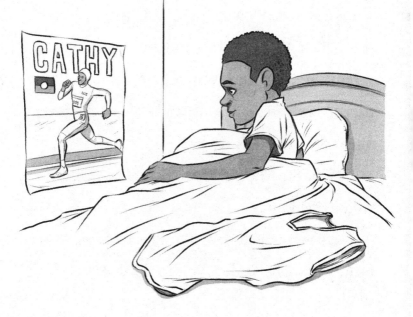

CHAPTER

12

MY YEAR FIVE CLASS and the year sixes and sevens all came to watch our semifinal. Our parents were in the stands, and so were the parents of the St. Michael's players.

"Go, St. Mary's!" our parents called out as we warmed up.

Tyson nudged me in the shoulder. "Good luck, Patty," he said. "We can do this."

Coach Clarke called us into the huddle minutes before the game started. "This is what we've been training for all season. I believe you can win this game if you try your very best and play as a team."

We were all listening to him as though our lives depended on it. He continued, "For the first five minutes of the game, I want you to try and beat St. Michael's with speed. Tyson and Patty, bring the ball up quickly, and don't be afraid to cut straight through the traffic to score."

He paused for a second and then asked, "Everyone feeling all right?" We all sized up the St. Michael's players. They were the runners-up to our team the year before, but they looked much bigger than us. They seemed cool and collected.

We all nodded. "No matter what happens today," Coach told us, "you've all played well this season. I'm very proud of you all. Now go get 'em."

Josie, Tiago, Manu, Tyson and I ran onto the court as our schoolmates and parents cheered. Our teammates on the bench beat their feet on the floorboards. I could feel my heart pumping through my chest.

In the tip-off, the opposition got the ball. One of their players bolted down the court, received the pass and made an easy layup, even though Tiago was right on his heels.

That's not a good start, I thought.

I passed the ball in to Tyson and he started sprinting down the court with it. I kept pace across from him. He passed back to me and I ran flat out for the basket, weaving through the defense, hurriedly making a shot. The ball fell through the hoop and the crowd went nuts.

"Go, Patty," they screamed, and I could see Dad and Mum jumping out of their seats.

But the opposition dug in. As fast and clever as we played, we didn't seem to be able to keep up with St. Michael's. They kept us on the back foot with fake shots, and stole the ball at every opportunity.

St. Michael's' score kept climbing, but the next time Tyson and I brought the ball down, with two opposition players pushing up on us, we passed the ball back and forth to give ourselves more room, and finally Tyson was able to pass to

Tiago, who shot and scored. "Yes!" I said, and gave them both a pat on the back.

After St. Michael's scored their next basket, I was relieved when Coach Clarke called a time-out.

We drank from our water bottles as the coach addressed us.

"Tyson, come off. Boris, you play point guard, Patty, you assist. Our strategy hasn't worked so far, but our last play was a lot better. This time when you bring the ball down, pass to each other much quicker."

Boris and I tried to do exactly what Coach Clarke had recommended, but Josie missed a shot and so did Boris. The ball was turned over and St. Michael's scored two easy baskets.

That's when Coach Clarke subbed me off for Tyson. The score was fourteen to four and I was relieved to take a rest, but keen to get back out there and help turn the score around.

At halftime St. Michael's were twenty points to our ten. I hated being so far behind. But Coach Clarke still believed in us. He walked us over to sit under the basket and said, "I don't want you to think about the score or anything that happened in the first half. You have another half to play."

I looked at Tyson, his face covered with sweat. He looked wild.

"Come on, Tyson, you can turn this game around," I told him.

Tyson looked at us all. "*We* can do this," he said.

WHEN OUR TEAM stepped back onto the court, the crowd started yelling for us louder than ever. I was starting with Tyson, Josie, Manu and Boris.

Within a minute, Josie had scored. We all jumped up and I gave her a double high five.

"Let's push up on them, Patty and Manu," Tyson said when the ball went back to St. Michael's.

The two players trying to bring the ball down to their basket looked frustrated as we triple-teamed them. Manu stole the ball and sprinted to our basket. He shot, and we scored again.

When there were only four minutes remaining in the game, we needed two points to draw.

"Let's just pass back and forth to each other and whoever can make a shot makes it, okay?" Tyson told me.

"Sounds good to me," I replied, and we started our move toward the basket. By the time we'd gotten to the key, I was the one with the ball in my hands.

I spun around the player screening me and shot, just as one of their players pushed into me and I fell to the ground.

I didn't even need to look up to know that I had scored. Our supporters were going off, yelling, "Patty, Patty, Patty," and they shouted even louder when the referee called a foul.

I stood at the free throw line, about to take the most important shot of the season. The shot that could put us in front by a point with only two minutes to go.

I closed my eyes and tried to slow down my breathing. I thought about Cathy Freeman gathering her nerve before the biggest race of her life. "All I can do is my best," I told myself. I bounced the ball twice, hard, into the court, gripped it and then sprung up onto my toes, pushing my arm straight into the air and letting the ball roll off my index finger.

It bounced off the backboard, hit the hoop, and fell through the basket. The score was twenty-two to twenty-three. We were up by a point! Tyson came and slapped me on the back before turning to the rest of the team. "Cool down now," he said. "We have to focus."

St. Michael's were quick in their counter-attack, and within seconds they had scored. With just under a minute left on the clock, they were a point ahead of us once more.

Tyson sprinted toward our basket as if the two players pressing on him weren't even there. Then he hurled himself into the air, holding the ball in one hand and making a long pass to our basket.

It was like watching a pack form in football. Then everyone was leaping for it. Somehow Josie got her fingertips on the ball and tipped it in the basket.

She scored. Everyone went crazy.

The St. Michael's players sprinted back to the end of the court. Copying Tyson's move, they made a long pass – but I saw it coming and made a steal. I got my hands on the ball, but it was quickly plucked from my grip and their shooter dribbled out beyond the three-point line, turned and shot.

The screaming of the St. Michael's supporters was deafening as the shot fell through the hoop.

I looked up at the scoreboard. There were only two seconds left on the clock.

Coach Clarke called time-out. *What's the point?* I thought.

I looked at my teammates, who all appeared on the verge of tears. I felt the same way.

"We've got two seconds left and one more play," Coach said. "But I just want to remind you that no matter what happens in the next two seconds, you've done yourselves, your team, me and the school proud. You can all hold your heads up high."

I waited anxiously for Coach Clarke's game plan. I had no idea how we could win.

"Tyson, I want you to pass the ball to Tiago. Tiago, you have such a strong arm. As soon as you get the ball, shoot it from wherever you are on the court. Everyone else, get ready for the rebound. If you get one, try to tip it in."

As soon as Tiago got the ball he took a shot. I positioned myself for the rebound, but the ball bounced off the hoop and into the hands of one of the St. Michael's players.

And the siren sounded.

"No!" I yelled. Josie gave me a hug, but the smile on Coach Clarke's face was the only thing that told me losing wasn't the end of the world.

Heavyhearted, we shook the hands of the St. Michael's players and congratulated them.

Afterward, I sat on the bench alone, looking up at the scoreboard and feeling like I'd let my team down.

Coach Clarke huddled us up. "We can't change the outcome," he said. "We can only learn from it."

"If only I was better, if only I was as good as the rest of you, and taller," I said.

"It's not your fault we lost, Patty," Boris told me.

"You played a great game, Patty. And you improved the whole way through the season."

"Yeah, you've become an awesome part of the team," Manu said.

DESPITE THEIR COMFORTING WORDS, for days all I could think about was losing our semifinal. I was so down that Dad almost had to drag me to dance practice. When I started dancing, though, I thought about how good it felt to be part of a team, all knowing the moves and working together, feeding off each other's energy. And

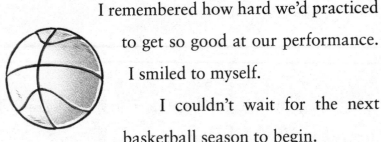

I remembered how hard we'd practiced to get so good at our performance.

I smiled to myself.

I couldn't wait for the next basketball season to begin.

GLOSSARY

AFL: Australian Football League. Often used to refer to Australian Rules (Aussie rules) football as a sport.

athletics: skills like running, jumping and throwing. Commonly referred to as track and field.

back pocket: a defender position in Australian Rules (Aussie rules) football in front of the other team's goal. The player's job is to try and stop goals from being scored by the other team.

backline: defender positions in Australian Rules (Aussie rules) football where the job of the players is to try and stop the other team from scoring.

basketballer: basketball player.

boot: kick. "Boot through it" means to kick the ball hard.

center half-forward: an offensive position in Australian Rules (Aussie rules) football where the player moves midway between the goal and the middle of the field. The player's job is to try and score goals and to help other players to score.

change rooms: locker rooms.

cheeky: playful or mischievous.

cricket: a game played with a hard ball and flat bat on an oval grass field. It started in England.

dish it off: pass the ball.

drop punt: kicking the ball on the pointed end so it spins (in Australian Rules football).

first light: when the sun rises.

footballer: football player.

footy: short for football. "Footy" means the game of Australian Rules (Aussie rules) football and the ball itself. The ball and the field are oval shaped.

forward: an offensive player in team sports, including Australian Rules (Aussie rules) football.

full-forward: an offensive position in Australian Rules (Aussie rules) football in front of the goal where the player's job is to kick goals.

get a go: have a chance.

grand final: the last game in a championship series.

handball: to pass the ball to another player in Australian Rules (Aussie rules) football by holding it with one hand and punching it with the other hand.

have a go/have a try: take a chance; give it a try.

holding the ball: a common call in Australian Rules (Aussie rules) football that people often disagree about. It is called when a player does not correctly get rid of the football when they are tackled.

holidays: vacation.

kept on the back foot: not strong or confident.

kick a bag of goals: kick a lot of goals.

kick-to-kick: a fun version of Australian Rules (Aussie rules) football played in the backyard or park by two or more people. One person kicks the football and another marks the ball.

lounge room: living room.

make a try: a way of scoring points in rugby.

mark: to catch the ball in the air before it touches the ground in Australian Rules (Aussie rules) football.

meter: 100 centimeters, about 39 inches.

netball: a game like basketball that is played with a ball similar to a soccer ball. "Netball" also means the ball used to play the game.

NRL: National Rugby League. Often used to refer to rugby league as a sport in Australia.

on the ball: a player who follows the ball on the field, rather than staying in one spot.

oval: a playing field or sports field for Australian Rules (Aussie rules) football and other sports, including cricket.

revision: studying, correction and extra work.

rover: a position in the middle of the field in Australian Rules (Aussie rules) football. The player's job is to try and clear the ball out from the center after the umpire bounces the ball to start or restart the game at any time in the match.

ruck: a position in Australian Rules (Aussie rules) football where the player's job is to try and tap the ball to a rover when the umpire has bounced the ball to start or restart the game at any time in the match. Similar to the start of a basketball game.

rugby: a game similar to rugby league. It started in England.

scratch match: scrimmage or practice game.

share [it] around: share with others.

sportspeople: athletes.

three-quarter time: the break between the third and fourth quarters in Australian Rules (Aussie rules) football.

Torres Strait: the waters and group of islands between Australia and Papua New Guinea, the traditional home of Torres Strait Islander people. Australia has two Indigenous groups, Aboriginal and Torres Strait Islander.

Torres Strait Islander: Torres Strait Islander people, Indigenous to Australia.

year five class: fifth grade class. Year six and seven are sixth and seventh grade.

PATTY MILLS was born in Canberra. His father is from the Torres Strait Islands, and his mother is originally from the Kokatha people in South Australia. Patty plays with the San Antonio Spurs in the NBA and is a triple Olympian with the Australian Boomers (Beijing '08, London '12, Rio de Janeiro '16).

JARED THOMAS is a Nukunu person of the Southern Flinders Ranges. His novels include *Dallas Davis, the Scientist and the City Kids* for children, and *Sweet Guy, Calypso Summer* and *Songs that Sound Like Blood* for young adults. Jared's writing explores the power of belonging and culture.